For K, my endless source of inspiration.

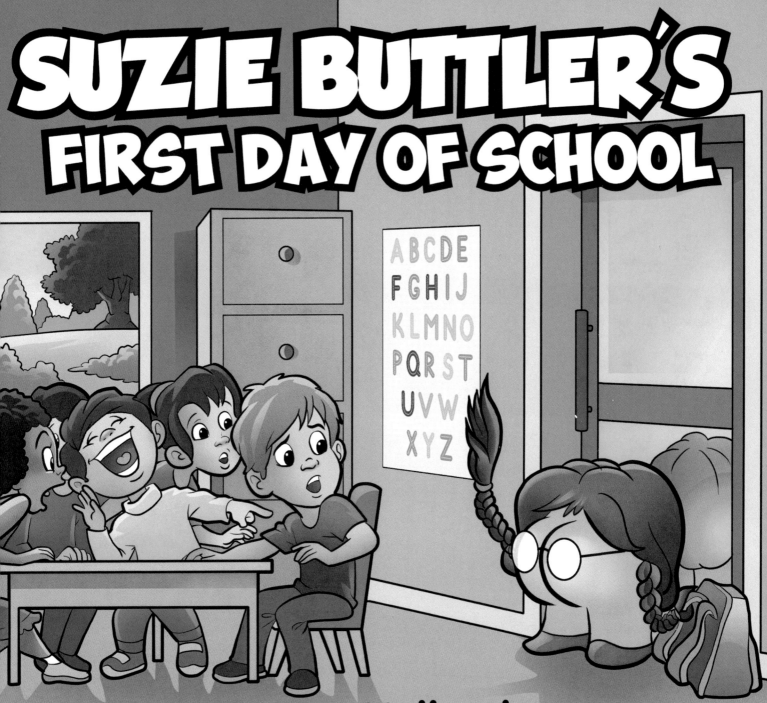

SUZIE BUTTLER'S
FIRST DAY OF SCHOOL

Brett Van Valkenburg
Illustrated by Sona & Jacob

Suzie Buttler lived in an apartment in New York City with her parents and brother. In many ways, Suzie was just like every other little girl, except for one thing...

Suzie was a
rear-end.
A bum!
A booteus
maximus!
A BUTT.

It was the last day of August, and Suzie was excited because the next morning was the start of her very first day of kindergarten.

"I've got my lunchbox, my notebook, and my pencils. This is gonna be great!" she said.

The next morning a bus came to bring the Buttler kids to school.

"Don't think you're sitting with me," said Harold. "I don't want people to think we're related."
"I'd rather sit on a bloated porcupine than sit with you," Suzie replied.

Just when Suzie thought that no one wanted to sit with her, she heard a voice from overhead. "You can sit with me if you want," said a little girl.

"I'm Cindy," said the girl. "Thanks. I'm Suzie."

At the beginning of class, the teacher, Miss Netty, had each student say their name and something they did that summer.
Suzie thought she heard some of the children giggling when it was her turn.

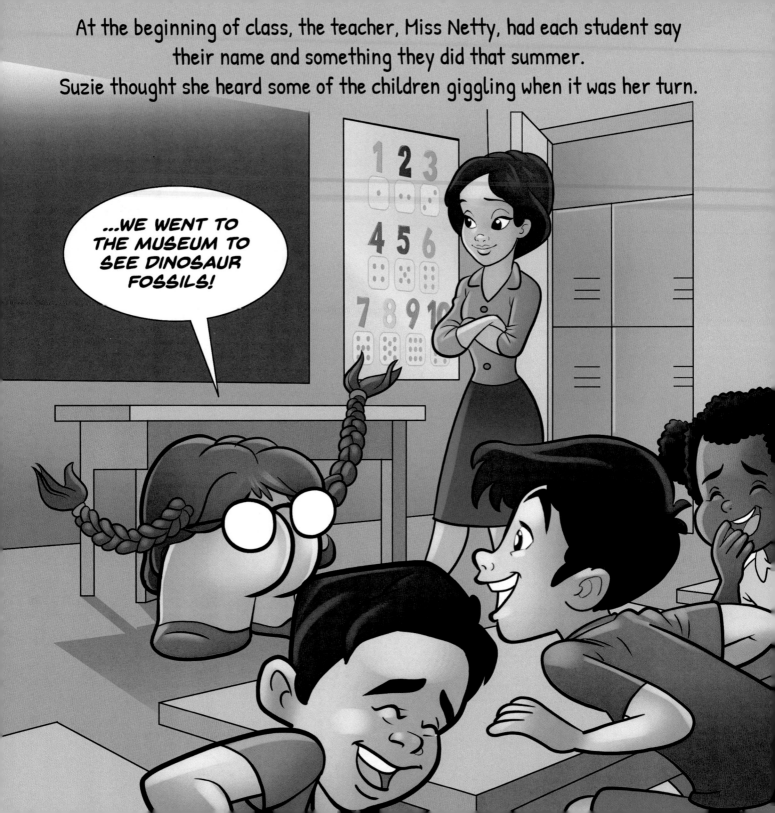

Playtime came, but no one wanted to play with Suzie.

Except for Cindy.

Lunchtime came, but no one wanted to sit with Suzie.

Except for Cindy.

Suzie enjoyed playing all the different instruments during music class.

But when it was Suzie's turn to play the pennywhistle, Tommy grabbed it from her. "Hey, it's my turn!" said Suzie. "I'm not blowing on this thing after it's been in *your* mouth!" he said. "Yuck!"

The children began to laugh. Suzie had enough of the kids being mean to her. She left the group and went to the class library.

Where she sat down and
began to cry.

Miss Netty could see Suzie was upset. "Children, let's play a little game," she said. "Form teams based on your class tables. Whichever team can build the highest Lego tower wins."

"Suzie, don't let anyone tell you that who you are is wrong. You are a kind, bright little girl, and that's what really matters."

Suzie stopped crying. "Thanks," she said. "Now, do you want to come out and play?" said Miss Netty. "I think your team could really use your help."

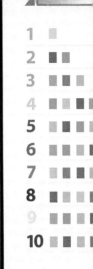

"We can't make this dog-gone thing any taller," cried James. "We're going to lose!"

With Suzie's help, her team quickly built a mighty tower.

The other children
could hardly believe it.
They had been beaten
by Suzie.

"Hooray for
Suzie!"
shouted
Suzie's
teammates.

At 3 o'clock school ended, and it was time to go home.

"You still can't sit with me," said Harold.

"I'll have plenty of places to sit," Suzie replied.

"Yeah, right," said Harold.

"Thanks," said Suzie, "but I'm going to sit with my new friend Cindy."

THE END